Running Deer
Plays Hooky

Arturo Muñoz Vásquez
Illustrated by Sonya Fe

dedicated to Simeon Mazatl Vásquez
who will always be my number one deer.

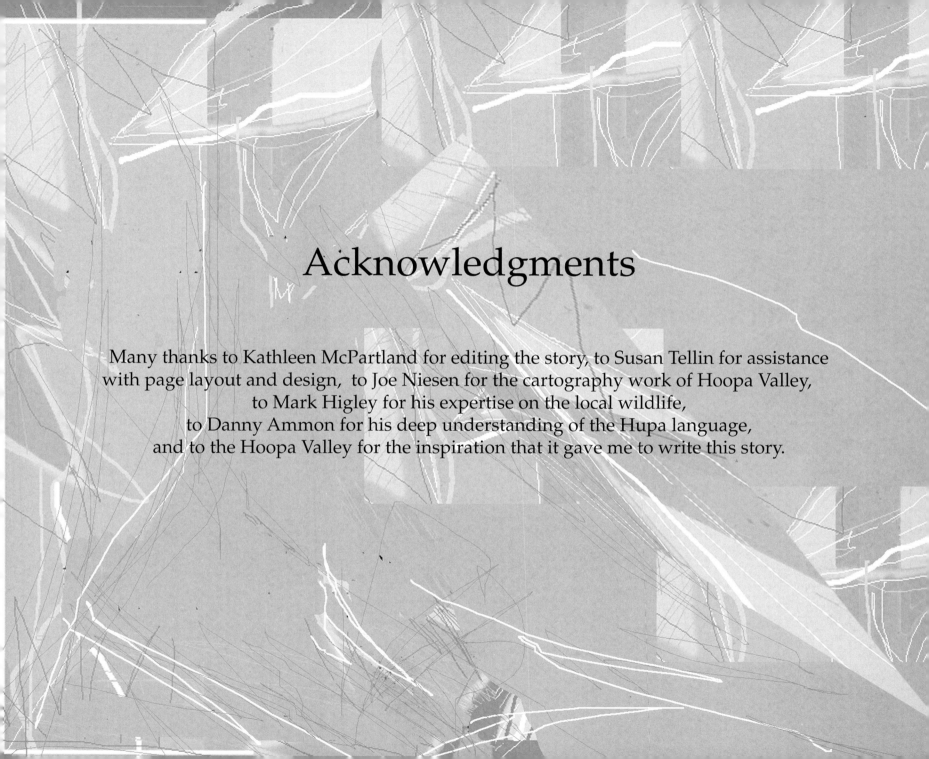

Acknowledgments

Many thanks to Kathleen McPartland for editing the story, to Susan Tellin for assistance with page layout and design, to Joe Niesen for the cartography work of Hoopa Valley, to Mark Higley for his expertise on the local wildlife, to Danny Ammon for his deep understanding of the Hupa language, and to the Hoopa Valley for the inspiration that it gave me to write this story.

Design and layout by Sonya Fe Studios

A seven year-old Native American student named Running Deer
is not able to read at the beginning of second grade.
To avoid the humiliation of failure to read in front of his peers,
Running Deer plays hooky; cuts school and hikes up the creek.
He encounters the wife and son of Bigfoot;
the old man from the forest; Tintah K' iwingxoya:n.
Running Deer learns to read nature from them.
He returns to school ready to learn to read from a book.

Literacy Activities are provided as an appendix.

Library of Congress Cataloging in Publication Data.

ISBN 0-9741971-0-6

Vasquetzal *Publishing*

Running Deer
Plays Hooky

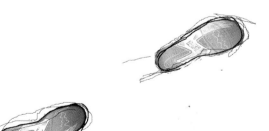

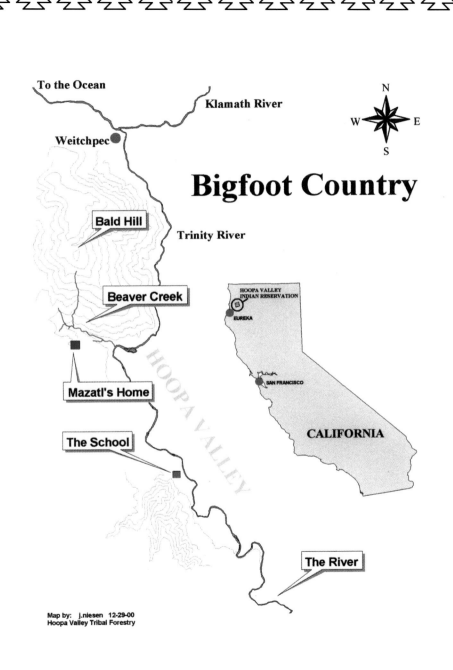

To the Ocean

Klamath River

Weitchpec

Bigfoot Country

Bald Hill

Trinity River

Beaver Creek

Mazatl's Home

The School

HOOPA VALLEY
INDIAN RESERVATION

EUREKA

SAN FRANCISCO

CALIFORNIA

HOOPA VALLEY

The River

Map by: j.niesen 12-29-00
Hoopa Valley Tribal Forestry

*I*n the mountains of the north eastern part of Humboldt county where the Trinity and Klamath rivers meander with long and lazy turns, lived an Indian boy named K'itixun dahch' idiwinLa:t, which means running deer in Hupa, his native language. His family and friends called him Running Deer.

In the mornings, Running Deer arrived at the bus stop, as he did every morning, way before everyone did. He was always first in line. He liked going to school. He liked playing with other children and with the toys in his classroom. He liked the flash card games he played with Mrs. Parrish. At the end of first grade Running Deer was a happy boy.

Running Deer began having problems in school when he entered second grade; the grade where children are expected to read. He enjoyed school when the teacher read to the class; she made the stories seem so real. The part of the school day that he didn't enjoy was when he was asked to read in front of the entire class. He continued to struggle sounding out some of the letters of the alphabet. And with some words, he did not even have a clue as to where to begin to sound out the group of letters on the flash cards. The sentences on the page looked more like rivers, creeks, and mountains to him. When he stumbled on sounding them out, some kids would laugh. He'd thought of running and hiding so no one would see him cry.

He also didn't like silent reading. He wondered how he could be expected to read a book without any help. He looked at the pictures as he pretended to read. He moved his lips to make it look as though he was reading.   "I can't read," he thought.

By the end of the winter, Running Deer was no longer the first one at the bus stop, nor did he compete to be first in line. He was falling behind in reading. The more he struggled with reading, the more the children laughed at him, and the farther back in line he stood. He was no longer racing everywhere; instead, he walked to where he needed to go.

One morning, Running Deer did not get on the school bus to go school. Instead he decided he was going to skip school and play hooky all day. That day he walked up Beaver Creek until he was too tired to walk any further. He sat down and leaned his back against a tree trunk and thought about how he'd rather be with his friends at school. He got up and hiked for another hour. Finally, he stopped and climbed on top of a boulder when he heard, "Oh, Oh!" Someone was crying.

Running Deer leaned quietly over the boulder to see who was crying. He noticed that a bear cub had caught its foot in a metal trap. The cub tried to pull its foot out of the trap and cried, "ayee". His ankle was bleeding. The poor cub was in a lot of pain. Running Deer climbed down to help. The bear cub was in so much pain that he didn't notice Running Deer reach down and with a stick pry open the trap. Startled, the cub pulled his foot free with a happy cry, " 'aaow."

Suddenly, the bear cub fought as if he was being attacked. Running Deer jumped back and started to run when he heard the cub call out, "Wait, I thought you were going to hurt me. I thought you were a hunter coming to check on the trap."

"No! I just came down to help. I saw that you were hurt. Your ankle must really hurt, huh?" asked Running Deer at the same time realizing that he was talking to a bear. *Impossible*, he thought.

"Yeah! it really hurts. Listen, my name is Nosy, but my mother calls me Baby."

"My name is K'itixun dahch' idiwinLa:t, in Hupa it means running deer. Wait a minute! Since when can bears talk?" he asked. He cleaned the cub's foot and helped him into the creek to washed off the rest of the blood. The cub also washed the mud off his face.

"Hey! Your face is the same color as mine. Why? You're human too?" exlaimed Running Deer.

"Don't be scared, my mother can explain. Please help me walk back to her circle?" asked Nosy.

"Sure... but...where do you need to go?" asked Running Deer.

"That way *Púufich Ukviipti*! That means Running Deer in Karuk," pointed Nosy. As Nosy limped along, Running Deer helped him walk. Nosy cried "Aahh!", each time he placed too much weight on his injured foot.

They had walked only a short distance when they were attacked by a big angry black bear. For a frozen moment Running Deer thought he was going to die.

"No! Mother!" yelled Nosy stopping the attack. "He saved my life. He freed my foot from a trap," Nosy kept on yelling, "No!" He knew how vicious his mom could be if her Baby was in danger of being hurt.

"Baby, are you all right?" asked Mama Bear with concern as
she picked Nosy up and walked off with him in her arms.

" Running Deer used a stick to free my foot from a bear trap. Next time, I'll use a stick to free my foot from a trap."

"No, Baby! There's not going to be a next time," threatened Mama Bear.

"OK! Mama. Running Deer cleaned my wound and helped me walk up stream. He saved my life."

"So, you saved Baby's life, huh?" asked Mama Bear inspecting the hero, then inviting him to walk with them. Running Deer noticed that even a big ferocious black bear could cry. As her tears ran down her cheeks, the tears wiped off mud from her face exposing the light skin underneath. She too had a human face. *How odd,* thought Running Deer, *the talking bears have human faces.* Mama Bear knew what Running Deer was thinking, "Yes, we have faces, feelings, and we talk and walk like humans."

"Are you?" Running Deer started to ask with a puzzled look.

"Yes, and we are related to the bears too. You see, the people from around here and bears have a common ancestor. That is why the Hupa call us, *Tintah K' iwingxoya:n the old man of the forest.* We darken our faces with mud to hide better in woods. We are afraid of humans. In the forest, we have the superior ability to camouflage ourselves. We hide during the day and come out at night. That's how we've learned your ways and languages. I've learned enough from them to fear that one day, Baby will be caught and skinned alive."

"Baby likes to wander off and sometimes he goes down the creek too far, like he did today." Nosy had fallen asleep in Mama's arms, she gently nestled him down on a grassy bed. She watched her son; she wrinkled her nose to smell the air, listened to the wind, and looked down the mountain for the hunters. At the moment, all was safe.

"Come to think of it. Why are you not in school?" asked Mama Bear.

"I don't like school," said Running Deer lowering his head.

"Why don't you like school?" asked Mama Bear, getting closer.

"The kids laugh at me because I can't read," answered Running Deer with sadness in his voice.

"Everybody can read," said Mama Bear with the strong conviction of a reading teacher. She reached down and pulled on Running Deer's arm, inviting him for a walk.

"I will show you that you can read, but it will take work on your part. Come, walk with me a ways."

They climbed to a nearby vista point. "Stand there and close your eyes. Read with your nose." A few moments went by. "Now tell me, what can you read?" asked Mama Bear.

At first, Running Deer didn't know what she meant by read with your nose. Just then, a strong scent of sap from a Douglas fir reached his nose, "I read tree sap!" he exclaimed. He went on reading with his nose. He was excited to know he could actually read something. Though it wasn't the same kind of reading that he learned at school, it was reading. *I can read,* he thought.

Running Deer would remember that moment for the rest of his life. He was excited to go home and prepare for his return visit with his new friends. He arrived at the bus stop and interacted with the rest of the kids. He noticed that no one had missed him at school nor at home. After that first day playing hooky, he played hooky again, and no one noticed his absence, not the bus driver, nor his teacher.

At school, he had become talkative and disruptive. His teacher saw him as defiant and lacking respect for adults. The teacher did not miss telling him, "Pay attention and do your work!" Since the teacher did not mark him absent on the school attendance reports, the school secretary didn't find out about his absences, hence the school did not notify Running Deer's parents of his absence.

Every morning, he dressed and carried his backpack to the bus stop. At the bus stop, he visited with his friends before sneaking away, hoping that by making bus stop appearances, he would not be missed at school.

He hiked up Beaver Creek to visit with Nosy and Mama Bear. He even visited them when it was raining.

Mama Bear taught Running Deer to read the pungent odor of ants in a decaying log and the smell of a fire scar on an old black oak tree. After many lessons, Running Deer learned to distinguish the smell of a deer from one of a bear. He learned to pick up the distinct smell of a human. Mama Bear made reading fun and Running Deer was eager to learn.

In early Spring, Mama Bear informed Running Deer that he was going to learn another way to read. He became very excited about learning a different way to read nature. He knew that it had something to do with his senses: either his eyes, ears, or mouth. Mama Bear was teaching him to read nature with his senses. He had learned to use his sense of smell to read. He learned to sniff the air for clues.

"Well, K'itixun dahch' idiwinLa:t, do you know what the new reading technique of the day is?" asked Mama Bear.

"Reading with my ears! Right?" he asked while at the same time seeing Nosy rub his ears with his hands. Having learned to be observant, Running Deer had seen Nosy's cue.

"Yes, today, you will learn to read with your ears. Now, be still and listen. Close your eyes again, hold your breath and read with your ears. Don't let the sound of your heart beat interfere with the other noises in the air."

Running Deer closed his eyes and listened. He sniffed the air.

"No, don't read with your nose this time. Just use your ears. Focus on hearing the full range of sounds, from the loudest to the faintest, " said Mama Bear.

"I can read the bird in the tree because it is the loudest."

"Yes, that's the scolding of Steller's jay," added Mama Bear.

"I can read the sounds made by the running water in the stream. I can read the high pitch chirp of a chipmunk and the tapping of a western gray squirrel's front foot. Oh! I can read the heavy hammering of a pileated woodpecker. I can read the whistle in the wind," he expounded with his eyes tightly closed. Running Deer learned to read quickly with his ears. "What bird made that call, Mama Bear?" he asked with enthusiasm.

"Open your eyes, now. See the red scalped woodpecker flying over us, well you just heard its raucous laughing call." Mama Bear and Running Deer laughed as Nosy mimicked the bird call.

By Mid-Spring, Mama Bear introduced reading with his eyes, "This reading technique is the hardest to learn because your nose and ears get in the way. You must learn to tune them out and later when you can read with your eyes, then you can use your ears and nose to see the whole picture," making a large circle in the sky with her hairy arms. "Do you understand?" she asked.

"I think so," added Running Deer.

With a serious teacher's voice, Mama Bear instructed, "Now, read things up close. Look for small things: ants, grains of sand, and the small holes in the acorns," said Mama Bear with a serious voice.

Running Deer was too busy reading the small things at his feet to respond: ants walking through blades of grass. He noticed that they were carrying something. "Are those eggs they're carrying?" he asked.

"Yes, the morning rain flooded their ant colony. Now they are trying to relocate their colony to higher ground."

Nosy read along with Running Deer's lessons. While he was still too young for some of them, he practiced reading anyway. The three of them read the signs for rain in the dark clouds. "Well, it looks like it's about to rain," said Nosy with some assurance. The light rain filled the air with fresh reading material.

In the weeks that followed, Running Deer learned to read the tracks of fisher, gray fox, ringtail cat, deer, mountain lion, gray squirrel, mice, and snakes. He also practiced scanning the forest, focusing on one tree, and zooming in on the bird in its branch. These exercises were teaching him to read nature's clues. He developed a keen vision too.

One late Spring day when he was hiking near the school, he scanned the winding road below. He saw a green truck heading towards the school. Running Deer sniffed the air, listened attentively, and scanned the activity below. The two forest rangers were looking for something or someone. Mama Bear had taught him to read nature and to see with all his senses. He concluded that perhaps they were looking for him.

Sometime in the summer, when he should have been in summer school, instead he was in the meadows of Bald Hill, Mama Bear and Nosy prepared for a celebration: in an open pit she had cooked salmon on a stick, she had gathered a basket of huckleberries.

Mama Bear was wearing a pink apron. She looked real pretty; she had rubbed some black berries on her cheeks to give her light-skinned face a little color.

"Mama Bear, you look very pretty," said Running Deer giving her a hug.

"Thank you Ro up ue Puuek, that is your name in Yurok. *Now that you have learned your name in three of the many spoken languages of the forest, you are ready to re-enter the real world.* I'm dressed this way to honor your intellectual and spiritual development-your vision quest. Do you know what I am talking about?" asked Mama Bear.

"I've learned to read?" he answered.

"Yes, that's right and now you must go back to school. Learn to read from books," said Mama Bear with sadness in her eyes. "No more playing hooky for you. You must get serious about your school work. You have to work to make your dreams come true."

To Running Deer's surprise, he was not sad. He knew this time would come. He would miss them. Mostly, he would miss playing with Nosy. "I'll see you on weekends," he said.

"No, Ro up ue Puuek, you can't come back to visit us any more," cried Nosy. "Tell him why he can't, Mama!"

"What about this summer, when school is over?" interrupted Running Deer in desperation. "Can I visit then?" he begged for permission.

"I'm sorry K'itixun dahch' idiwinLa:t! To protect Mama Bear and me, you must stay away," cried Nosy." "You can not visit us anymore, the hunters will follow you and eventually they will find us. Please, this is very hard for Baby and me. You must stay away," cried Mama Bear, tears rolled down her face. "Carry us in your heart," she said with bitter wisdom.

"You mean, I will never see you again?" he asked, knowing the answer. "Does this mean that I can not even talk about you and Nosy?"

"That's Right! K'itixun dahch' idiwinLa:t. Well," she reconsidered, "if you must talk about us 'bears,' tell them not to kill us because we are their 'grandfathers'." They gave each other bear hugs, and then the three of them embraced.

Running Deer respected her wishes and in September he enrolled in third grade. His friends had become nicer. Running Deer was still having reading problems. Something important had changed, the girls and boys didn't laugh at him anymore. They saw him try very hard to read, so they helped him.

On Fridays, Running Deer began having lunch with a high school tutor, who was a basketball player. Sometimes, instead of having lunch in the cafeteria, they walked around school. They told each other stories. Running Deer taught his tutor new games; how to read with his ears, eyes, and nose. He liked laughing with him. Running Deer enjoyed reading to him. His tutor didn't correct him every time Nosy stumbled, only when Nosy asked for help.

Running Deer liked reading to the Reading Recovery lady too. He called her the Railroad Lady because the box she carried from classroom to classroom had a railroad crossing sign drawn on it; two big R's written inside a yellow diamond shape.

The Railroad Lady and Running Deer would find a place to cut words out and organize them into sentences. Once he placed them in a sequence, he would read the story to the Railroad Lady. Running Deer wanted to learn to read; he wanted to learn about the stories the letters and words made when he read them. He read with more success each week, until he advanced enough not to need special help. At about the same time, he no longer needed tutoring, in fact, his tutor was now helping another student.

By late spring, Running Deer had learned to read and liked going to school again. Once again, he was first at the bus stop. In June, after school had finished with testing, they had their annual Literacy Faire. Running Deer was selected to read his blue ribbon book, "Our Grandfathers," to ninety-three second and third graders. Running Deer remembered Mama Bear's lessons, "read with all your senses."

"*Our Grandfathers*, written and illustrated by Running Deer," he read. As the words came out of his mouth, he sniffed the air, listened for noises, and looked beyond the sea of faces. While he read his story, he thought of his secret friends, proof that *the old man of the forest* had a family, Mama Bear and Nosy. He finished reading the last sentence of the story, "Remember not to kill the bears, for they are *our grandfathers!*" The short silence erupted into thunder from the applause, cheers echoed through the air, and from outside the auditorium, the high pitch sound waves of animal squeals reached the podium. The squeals were audible only to trained ears.

When the clapping subsided, he was still reading with his senses; he heard noises coming from the wooded area outside the auditorium, and his nose picked up the strong odor of two black bears. Running Deer looked out through the opened door and saw Mama Bear and Nosy hiding under some trees. They were waving at him. He wanted to wave back, but instead he looked down to close his book, and by the time he looked up again, they were gone.

Running Deer walked back to his seat thinking, *I can read.*

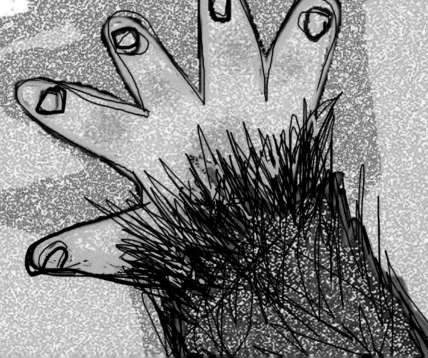

The End

Literacy Activities

Recall:

1) Where did the story take place?
2) Name two rivers that were mentioned in the story.
3) Name three characters.
4) What was Running Deer's name in Hupa, Yurok, or Karuk?

Process:

5) Compare Running Deer's school experience in first grade with the one in second grade.
6) Constrast Running Deer's feelings to where he stood first in line.
7) What happened that made Running Deer turn and become defiant and disruptive in class?

Synthesis:

8) Why did Running Deer play hooky?
9) How do you feel when people laugh at you?
10) What evidence in the story tells us that Mama Bear and Nosy were created by Running Deer's imagination?

Writing prompts:

11) Write a story that takes place in Hoopa Valley.
12) Write your own story about Big Foot.
13) Write your own story about why one might play hooky.
14) Write another chapter to Running Deer Plays Hooky.
15) Write your own story about the difficulty of learning to read.

About the Artist:

Fifth in a family of eight children, Sonya Fe grew up in a Los Angeles housing project known as *"Dogtown"* where life was tough and money was scarce. Even under these conditions, her talent as an artist became apparent early in her life. The young artist received encouragement from her parents and siblings. The cement floor of their home became her first drawing surface. Every day a new drawing in chalk was created for family amusement and every night her canvas would be mopped clean by her mother.

At the age of 13, Sonya won her first art scholarship to attend a summer program at Otis Art Institute in Los Angeles. Sonya Fe received her BA degree in art at the Art Center College of Design in Los Angeles. Sonya Fe's art has enjoyed a considerable amount of popularity in Hispanic-American Movement. Sonya Fe will be one of the featured artists in the soon to be released book, *The Contemporary Chicana and Chicano Art: Artist, Works, Culture, and Education* published by Bilingual Review/Press, Arizona State University. Sonya Fe has been published in many magazines and periodicals, and television coverage has followed her as she moved about the country. She has been featured in many art exhibits throughout the United States and Europe. Her work can be found in numerous private and public collections.

Sonya Fe teaches art for the College of the Redwoods in Hoopa, California. She works as an art consultant in school districts throughout California. Sonya Fe co-founded Children Teaching Children Institute; a literacy invention process of integrating literacy, art and technology.

Visit Sonya Fe's website at *www.sonyafe.com*

About the Author:

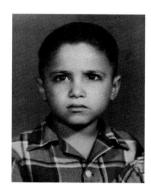

Arturo Muñoz Vásquez was born in Piedras Negras, Coahuila, México. When he was an infant, his family immigrated to the United States. The migratory life took him across western United States: to the apple orchards of Washington; to the potatoes fields in Idaho; and to the fruit orchards, the garlic and onion fields in Gilroy, California.

He has written the following stories: *Papá, Tell Us Another Story: A Collection of Bedtime Stories, A Storyteller's Nightmare: A Collection of Scary Stories, Where Are My Children: A Retold Story of La Llorona, Stories That You Can Read: Stories for Early Readers*, and *Add More Water to the Beans.* He enjoys telling his stories to students, teachers, and parents.

As an education consultant he provides professional development services to school districts on program improvement initiatives such as literacy interventions, system reform, bilingual education, and innovative ways to use categorical funding.

He has been a classroom teacher and wrestling coach in middle and high schools, a resource teacher in Migrant Education, an administrator in bilingual education and upward bound programs, an elementary school principal, a university professor, a bilingual/migrant consultant for the California Department of Education. He currently is the Superintendent for the Klamath-Trinity Joint Unified School District.

To employ him as an education consultant or a motivational speaker email him at vasquetzal@aol.com or purchase his books and cds: *www.vasquetzal.com.*